A
YELLOWSTONE

A B C

by Cyd Martin

ROBERTS RINEHART PUBLISHERS

A Little Rhino Book

To Kate, Case, and Jesse
who have grown up in Yellowstone
and to Steve, with love.

With special thanks to Sue Martin,
Rick and Jen Hutchinson,
and Wallis and Marianna Wimberley.

Copyright © 1992 by Cyd Martin
Published by Roberts Rinehart Publishers
P.O. Box 666, Niwot, Colorado 80544
International Standard Book Number 1-879373-12-2
Printed in Hong Kong

A is for antelope
their safety is in speed

B is for bison
who migrate in herds to feed

C is for coyote
pouncing on three mice

D is for Daisy Geyser
with eruptions quite precise

E is for elk
bugling in the fall

F is for Firehole River
fed by geysers large and small

G is for Grand Geyser
with ghost trees frosted white

H is for hawk
soaring at great heights

I is for iris
damp meadow dweller

J is for jays
both gray and Steller's

K is for kingfisher
diving for minnows

L is for lupine
blooming in bright meadows

M is for moose
hiding in the willows

N is for Norris Basin
where Steamboat Geyser billows

O is for Old Faithful
erupting nearly every hour

P is for Indian Paintbrush
a hardy western flower

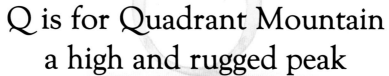

Q is for Quadrant Mountain
a high and rugged peak

R is for raven
with a pointed black beak

S is for Sandhill Cranes
returning every spring

T is for the Mammoth Terraces
made of travertine

U is for Ursus horribilis
the bear fishing in the stream

V is for volcanoes
that give the geysers their steam

W is for wolves
who lived here long ago

X is for the crisscross tracks
of animals in the snow

Y is for Yellowstone
where wilderness has a chance

Z is for zygogonium mats
where brine flies like to dance

Dear Reader,

Can you identify the small pictures in the borders of these pages? After you try, check here to see if you are correct!

Title page Indian paintbrush, Lower Falls, shooting star, bison, Old Faithful Geyser

A B   Aster, Buttercups

C D   Columbine, Chickadees

E F   Emerald Pool, Fire, Fireweed

G H   Great Blue Heron, Fringed Gentian

I J   Old Faithful Inn, Jackrabbit

K L   Lone Star Geyser, Larkspur

M N   Magpie, Clark's Nutcracker

O P   Calipso Orchid, Porcupine

Q R   Riverside Geyser, Wild Rose

S T   Tower Falls, Big Horn Sheep

U V   Ungulate Tracks, Vixen Geyser, Violets

W X   Woodland Star, Xerophyllum Tenax (beargrass)

Y Z   Yellowstone River, Zipper Creek

This page Pink Cone Geyser, glacier lily, antelope, iris, Grand Prismatic Spring

Glossary

Antelope: Antelope live in the northern part of Yellowstone. Their tan and white coloring is good camouflage and their speed helps to keep them safe from predators.

Bison: Hundreds of bison range throughout Yellowstone, traveling from the high country in the summer to the lower elevations in the winter. They sometimes walk out of the park in their search for grass to eat.

Coyote: Coyotes can often be seen hunting for mice in the grassy meadows of the park. When they spot one they will spring up in the air and catch the mouse with their front paws as they land.

Daisy Geyser: Daisy is found in the Upper Geyser Basin along the trail to Morning Glory Pool. Daisy erupts approximately every 100 minutes, shooting diagonally up into the air.

Elk: Thousands of elk live in Yellowstone. The male elk, or bulls, have large spreading antlers. In the fall the bulls challenge each other with a loud bugling call. They then joust with their antlers to establish who will gain control of the herds of females (cows). Another name for elk is wapiti.

Firehole River: The Firehole River runs through the Upper Geyser Basin, the Middle Geyser Basin, and on down to join the Gibbon River to form the Madison River. The Firehole is kept so warm by the water flowing into it from the geysers and hot springs that it never freezes, even during the ex-tremely cold periods of a Yellowstone winter.

Grand Geyser: Grand Geyser is the largest predictable geyser in Yellowstone. It erupts to a height of 200 feet every seven to ten hours. Grand Geyser is in the Upper Geyser Basin near Old Faithful.

Hawks: Many hawks are found in Yellowstone. Rough-legged hawks are found in the park during the winter when they migrate down from Canada. Hawks hunt for small mammals by circling high in the air and then diving down to catch them with their feet.

Iris: Wild iris bloom early in the summer and grow in meadow areas of the park that are moist. They can often be found in places where aspen grow along streams and ponds.

Jays: Gray jays and Stellar's jays live in Yellowstone and are famous for their courage in approaching people to beg for food. National parks are set aside so that the birds and animals can live undisturbed in their natural environment. These creatures should not be fed by people because it disrupts their normal way of life.

Kingfishers: Kingfishers are birds that live along streams and get their food by fishing for minnows in the water. When they spot a minnow they will dive down and grab it in their beaks.

Lupine: Lupine, a member of the pea family, blooms throughout Yellowstone in sunny areas and can often be seen right along the roadside. Lupine is most often lavender but can also be white or pink.

Moose: Moose are very large animals that prefer to live near lakes and marshy areas in Yellowstone. They like to eat willows and other plants that grow beside and in streams and ponds. They can sometimes be seen swimming quite long distances in the lakes in the park.

Norris Basin: Norris Geyser Basin is in the northern part of Yellowstone and is the most active thermal area in the park. Steamboat Geyser, the largest geyser in the world, is at Norris. Steamboat erupts to a height of 300 feet and has a spectacularly loud steam phase after the water bursts are finished.

Old Faithful: Old Faithful is the most famous geyser in Yellowstone. It erupts every 45 to 100 minutes, shooting water 180 feet into the air. It was named by the Washburn-Langford-Doane expedition in 1872 when they were amazed by the regularity of its eruptions.

Paintbrush: Indian Paintbrush is a common wildflower in the Rocky Mountains. The part of the plant that looks like the flower is actually a leaf part called a bract. Indian Paintbrush can be many different colors including red, orange, white, yellow, and a glorious bright pink. Indian Paintbrush is the state flower of Wyoming.

Quadrant Mountain: This mountain is visible to the west from the road between Norris and Mammoth Hot Springs.